for my DAD and BRUCE

With special thanks to Alix Reid, Edite Kroll, Martha Rago,
Kristin Daly, Michael Stearns, and Lorene Jean.

Library of Congress Cataloging-in-Publication Data   Becker, Suzy.   Manny's cows : the Niagara Falls tale / by
Suzy Becker.   p.   cm.   Summary: For his summer vacation, Manny takes his five hundred cows to Niagara Falls.
ISBN-10: 0-06-054152-0 (trade bdg.)   ISBN-13: 978-0-06-054152-1 (trade bdg.)   ISBN-10: 0-06-054153-9
(lib. bdg.) — ISBN-13: 978-0-06-054153-8 (lib. bdg.)   [1. Vacations—Fiction. 2. Cows—Fiction. 3. Niagara Falls
(N.Y.)—Fiction.] I. Title.   PZ7.B3817174Man 2006   2005014508   [E]—dc22   CIP   AC

Design by Martha Rago   1 2 3 4 5 6 7 8 9 10   ❖   First Edition

MANNY'S COWS

THE NIAGARA FALLS TALE

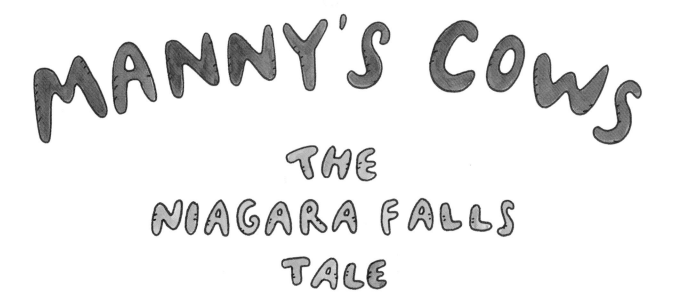

written and illustrated by

Suzy Becker

XZ

HarperCollins*Publishers*

Manny hated the last day of school.

"They should just cancel it," he grumbled.

"What are you doing for *your* summer vacation, Manny?"
Mrs. Kornitsky asked. The whole class looked at him.

"Well, you can't exactly *go* on vacation when you have five hundred cows," said Manny.

"What if you took them with you?" asked Mrs. Kornitsky. The class laughed.

"Hmm," Manny thought.

overnight camp?

Then he thought some more.

fishing?

And pretty soon, it was all he could think about.

I got it!!

"Bossy!" Manny yelled. Bossy met him at the end of the driveway.
"We're going on vacation!" Manny announced.

"Vacation?" She scratched the spot on the top of her head.

"We're going to see Niagara Falls!"

"See *who* do *what*?"
asked Bossy.

"Not who—just *what*,"
Manny said. "It's the
greatest tourist attraction
in the Northeast!

"The buses will be here tomorrow morning at six o'clock sharp," he
continued, "and we have a lot to do to get ready. I'm putting you in charge
of the cows!"

Ta·da·TA·DA·TA·DAAH!!!

"Charge!" Bossy yelled, and
she hightailed it through the
pasture.

Bossy rang her bell until the cows quieted down and all you could hear were the flies, the tall grass rustling in the breeze, and lots of chewing.

"Manny is taking us on vake-cake—er, a trip!"

The news was not well received.

Bossy rang her bell again. "We have less than twenty-four hours to get ready, so I suggest you zip up and pack up."

TIME to
GET UP!!!

In the morning, when the rooster crowed, the moon and the sun were both in the sky. Manny looked over at the barn. The cows were filing out to the buses with their bags trailing behind them. Everything was going according to plan!

The buses pulled out. "Oh no! I forgot my sunglasses!" said Beulah.

"I'm bus-sick," whined Flossie.

FACT:

CHEW
SPIT UP SWALLOW

Cows are constantly spitting up. *Cud* is the crud they chew,* swallow, spit up, chew, swallow, spit up, chew, swallow, spit up, chew, ad nauseam.

*A cow has zero front teeth up top.

"Are we there yet?" asked Buttercup.

"I don't care whether we ever get there!" Goldie exclaimed. "I am in love with these little TVs!"

"But I'm starving!" cried Clover.

Me TOOO!

Me THREE!

Me FOUR!

FACT:

Cows have not 1 but 4 stomachs. They eat about 100 pounds of food each day.

"EVERYONE SIT DOWN!" Manny shouted.

"How about a song?" Bossy suggested. "Singing can take your mind off all kinds of things."

She cleared her throat and began, "Old MacDonald had a farm, A-E-I-O-U! And on his farm he had a cow! A-E-I-O-U! With a *moo-moo* here . . ."

Buttercup led the second verse. "And on his farm he had a pig! A-E-I-O-U!"

All the cows joined in for the chorus:

They were halfway through the sheep verse when Manny
jumped up. The singing stopped.

"Pigs do NOT *moo-moo*.

"They *oink*. Sheep *baah*.

"And, for your information, roosters *cock-a-doodle-doo!*"
Manny sat back down.

The cows had never heard anything so hilarious in their
entire lives.

Manny couldn't take it anymore.
"Somebody stop this bus. I have
to get off!" he said.

They pulled in to the next rest area. With five
hundred hungry, thirsty, cooped-up cows, it
was NOT a quick stop.

By the time Manny got them all back in their seats, his cows were ready to nap.

The smell of warm milk and hay filled the air, and in spite of the racket, he fell fast asleep.

Manny didn't know how long the buses had been stopped when he opened his eyes. He sat up and shrieked, "MY COWS ARE ALL GONE!"

"Relax! We're right here," Bossy said. "But you could've warned us we were visiting the World's Biggest Faucet *before* we finished our super-size drinks."

FACT:

A cow drinks 30 gallons, or **500** glasses, of water a day.

"Oh no! Not *here*! THIS IS A STATE PARK!" Manny covered his eyes. "What about the ladies' room?"

He peeked. The line was a hundred cows deep. "Never mind."

When they were done, Manny counted the cows off by twos, threes, and fours. (He'd had enough Number One for that day.) "Wait! Somebody's missing!"

No one heard.

They were all on their tours.

Meanwhile Manny
searched low . . .

and high
for his missing cow.

He couldn't find
her anywhere.

"I GIVE UP!" he said
as he stomped onto the bus.

There she was!

"Come sit by me and watch TV!" said Goldie.

By the time he got Goldie out of her seat, the tours had wrapped up, and the cows had discovered the Official Gift Shop.

The cashier rang up the bill. Manny had not planned to buy a single gift. "This," Manny sputtered, "this is *not* a vacation!" The cows' ears twitched nervously. "THIS is a DISASTER!"

The cows tiptoed guiltily out of the shop.

"We have to help Manny get out of this mess," Bossy said.
They all put their heads together.

Manny stepped out of the shop just in time
to see Buttercup grab a barrel of milk, race to
the top of the falls, and . . .

FACT:

If you churn or shake cream for 15 minutes, it will turn into butter.

There was a stampede to the bottom.

Buttercup opened the barrel.
"Ladies"—she licked her hoof—"we're in the butter business!"

In no time at all, Manny's cows were up to their udders in orders for butter!

"Are you *the* Manny?" a happy customer asked. "You've raised some fine bovine! Next time Stan says he can't come camping on account of his cows, we'll just show him this picture, won't we, Irene?"

At the end of the day, Manny counted the money while his cows took down the stand. There was enough to pay for their mess . . .

. . . and ride home in style.

Bossy rested back on her elbows.

"Next summer we should go to Washington!"

"No, Hollywood!" shouted Goldie.

"The moon!" said Buttercup.

"Whatever happened to 'buffalo roam, cows stay home'?" Manny asked.

"Well, we're glad you didn't take the chickens," Bossy said. "Or the rooster!"

With that, they all croaked, "Baahkeedoinkledoo!" and got to laughing so hard, the limo wriggled as it went down the road.